Wonderfully, Perfectly Unusual!

A Story about Bullying

By Sharon Thayer
with Connor Thayer

Illustrated by Reuben McHugh
Backstory Illustrated by Andrew Smith

Always be the perfect you!
Sharon Thayer
2020

Wonderfully, Perfectly Unusual!

A Story about Bullying

Carousel Publishing, LLC
903-871-9872
sharon@Carousel-Publishing.com
www.Carousel-Publishing.com

Layout & graphics by Mary Alexander, MSA Design
Illustrations by Reuben McHugh, www.ReubenMcHughStudioLTD.com
Backstory illustrations by Andrew Smith, www.AndrewSmithArtist.myportfolio.com

LCCN: 2020916720

Publisher's Cataloging-In-Publication Data
(Prepared by The Donohue Group, Inc.)

Names: Thayer, Sharon, author. | Thayer, Connor, author. | McHugh, Reuben, illustrator. | Smith, Andrew (Andrew Edward), 1961- illustrator.
Title: Wonderfully, perfectly unusual! : a story about bullying / by Sharon Thayer with Connor Thayer ; illustrated by Reuben McHugh ; backstory illustrated by Andrew Smith.
Description: First edition. | [Tyler, Texas] : Carousel Publishing, 2021. | Interest age level: 004-008. | Summary: "Connor, a young great hammerhead shark pup, who is different from the other pups, learns how to deal with bullies. From the time he was born, Connor heard his mother describe him as 'wonderfully, perfectly unusual.' He soon learned that being unusual was the perfect way for him to be"--Provided by publisher.
Identifiers: ISBN 9781734030617 (softcover) | ISBN 9781734030648 (ebook)
Subjects: LCSH: Individual differences--Juvenile fiction. | Hammerhead sharks--Juvenile fiction. | Bullying--Juvenile fiction. | Friendship--Juvenile fiction. | CYAC: Individual differences--Fiction. | Hammerhead sharks--Fiction. | Bullying--Fiction. | Friendship--Fiction.
Classification: LCC PZ7.1.T44736 Wo 2021 (print) | LCC PZ7.1.T44736 (ebook) | DDC [E]--dc23

Printed in the United States.

My Dear Children,

Before you read *Wonderfully, Perfectly Unusual!* you might enjoy the backstory. You see, the backstory is the story that happened back before there was a story at all.

You will find the backstory at the back of the book.

Enjoy!

Ms. Sharon

Dedications

This book is dedicated to my grandson, who never hesitates to follow his passions, growing more wonderfully, perfectly Connor every day.

To my Kid Central kids, who were warned to never call me normal. I hope you have continued to discover your unique, amazing selves.

And to those of you just discovering your differences—polish them until they shine, and our world will be a brighter place.

Beneath the morning haze, Connor swam with his parents and his thirty-seven siblings. All the hammerhead shark pups looked and acted the same—except Connor.

When his brothers and sisters swam this way,
Connor swam that way.
When they went up,
he went down.

"He's RATHER UNUSUAL, don't you think?" asked an old gray shark who was swimming by.

Connor's mother smiled, held her head high, looked straight into his eyes, and said, "Thank you! Yes, he is." And with a loving nod she added, "Wonderfully, perfectly unusual."

Hearing the old shark's words made Connor sad, but his mother's words warmed his heart. He flipped into the air in his first ever loop-the-loop, feeling proud to be wonderfully, perfectly unusual.

Most young sharks love to eat shrimp and crabs—but not Connor. He didn't like meat. He preferred to eat plants. So, while the other sharks swam off to catch their dinner, Connor stayed behind, all alone, and munched on tasty sea plants.

“You’re SO WEIRD!” one of his brothers teased
as he circled around Connor.

Remembering what he had seen his mother do, Connor smiled, held his head high, looked straight into his brother's eyes, and said, "Thank you!"

Then, thinking "so weird" wasn't all that bad, Connor dove into a patch of turtle grass—his favorite breakfast.

A group of pups were playing hide-and-seek one morning—but not Connor. He headed off to explore. He was hoping to find a new friend so he wouldn't be so lonely, but instead he found a hidden cavern. Soon, it became his very own secret place.

From then on, each time he found a colorful piece of coral, Connor flipped it onto his forehead and carried it off to his cavern.

"You're NOT NORMAL!" a sleek girl shark
shouted when she spied him carrying
some pink coral.

Connor smiled, held his head high, looked straight into her eyes,
and said, "Thank you!"

As he swam off, he decided that "not normal"
was just fine with him. Then, he did a gentle loop-the-loop,
perfectly balancing his coral.

When they were tired, most of the sharks rested near the bottom of the lagoon—but not Connor. He preferred to rest in his secret cavern, surrounded by his treasures. Seeing him sneak off, a group of pups called out in loud, cruel voices, “You’re SO DIFFERENT!”

The words hurt at first, but Connor smiled anyway, held his head high, looked straight into their eyes, and said, “Thank you!” Then he flipped his tail and swam away, quite happy to be “so different.”

All the sharks in the lagoon liked to compete to see who was the fastest—but not Connor. He liked to swim slowly, collecting shells along the ocean floor. As he swam, the biggest shark called out in a nasty voice, "You're the STRANGEST SHARK IN THE OCEAN!"

Surprising the big shark, Connor smiled, held his head high, looked straight into his eyes, and said, “Thank you!”

Excited to be "the strangest shark in the ocean," he swam faster than usual, missing one perfectly beautiful shell.

One day, Connor noticed a girl shark twirling in the sea grass. He had never seen a shark twirl in the grass, especially such a beautiful one. Swimming closer, he said sweetly, “You are rather unusual.”

She smiled, held her head high, looked straight into Connor’s eyes, and said, “Thank you! Yes, I am.”

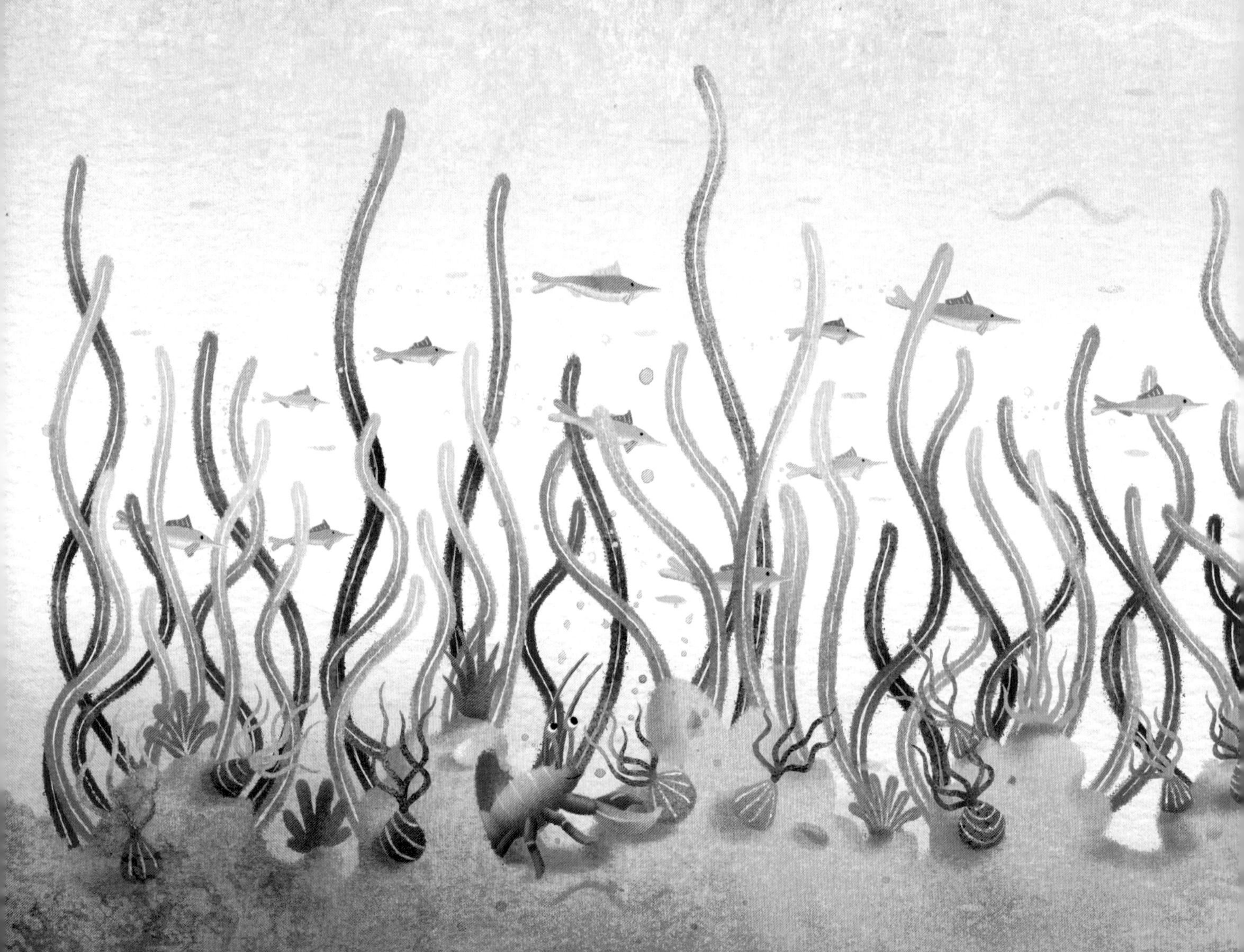

Connor smiled back. “Me too!”

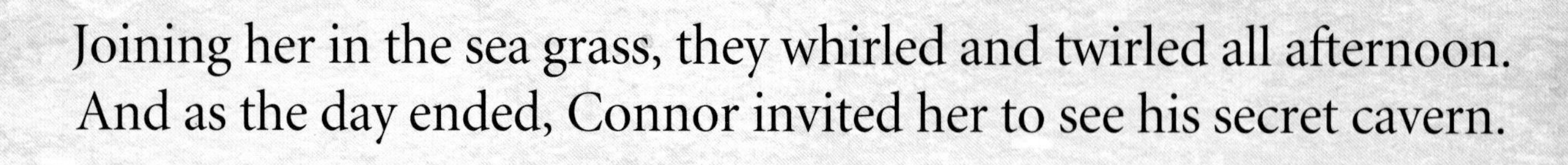

Joining her in the sea grass, they whirled and twirled all afternoon.
And as the day ended, Connor invited her to see his secret cavern.

Passing a crowd of young sharks, Connor heard them whispering
that they wished they, too, were a “little different,” or at least
not quite “so normal.”

Together, the two new friends burst into the air with spectacular loop-the-loops, celebrating how great it felt to be

A LITTLE STRANGE,

A LOT DIFFERENT, AND

WONDERFULLY, PERFECTLY UNUSUAL!

THE END

The Backstory of Wonderfully, Perfectly Unusual

After two years of being begged by my grandson to write a shark book, I found myself in the Caribbean Sea. I happily paddled my kayak along the shore, exploring the ecosystem where the endangered great hammerhead sharks live.

As I looked out at the horizon, I could not help but feel small in my kayak—but not as small as I was about to feel.

I was turning into a lagoon when a wave came from behind, tossing my boat about until I fell into the water. Pulled down by the currents, I tumbled over and over until I didn't know which way was up. Then, suddenly, the water became calm again. I quickly pushed toward the surface, gasping for air.

THE BACKSTORY

My kayak had drifted toward the land, leaving me behind. Luckily, there was a large rock nearby. I climbed on, thinking it would be a good place to catch my breath before swimming to shore.

Suddenly, two hands reached up toward the rock, followed by the head of a beautiful girl. At least, that's what I thought she was—until her fishtail splash behind her. I jerked back, too surprised to speak. I was staring at a mermaid!

"Please, don't swim through the lagoon," she said. "It's filled with sharks and their pups. If they think you're a threat to their babies, they might attack you. It's very dangerous. I'll stay with you while we wait for help, and I will tell you a story about a shark pup who was born in this lagoon."

THE BACKSTORY

Luna, the mermaid, told me funny tales all afternoon. Finally, we spied a fishing boat coming our way. She didn't want to be seen, but before she swam away, she made me promise to share the little shark's story with children everywhere.

A few minutes later, a fisherman named Esteban and his son helped me onto their boat and took me safely to shore. Esteban had been out on the sea teaching his son how to catch fish to feed their family.

THE BACKSTORY

Back at my cabin, I wrote down the story of the wonderfully, perfectly unusual shark, who I named Connor after my grandson. I hope you learn from Connor how wonderful it is to be yourself. No matter what that looks like, it will feel just right.

Through my travels, I've visited strange lands, with different people and unusual animals, but no matter where I've gone, many things have been the same. Both human and animal parents work hard to feed, protect, and teach their children how to get along in our world. When you look carefully, you'll see that beneath the differences, we are all quite the same.

As I head out in search of my next story, I hope to meet you along the way, chasing your own dreams. Wherever you are in the world, remember to go outdoors and explore, because you never know what you might find around the next corner.

Discover Great Hammerhead Sharks

There are more than 400 different kinds of sharks in the world. The smallest ones can fit in your hands and the largest ones are the biggest fish in the ocean. The first sharks lived about 450 million years ago. That's about 200 million years before dinosaurs!

Hammerhead sharks are just one type of shark, and the great hammerhead shark is the largest of all the hammerheads. It's an **endangered animal**, which means that there are very few of them alive and they could become extinct.

An **extinct animal** is when there are none alive anywhere in the world. All animals eventually become extinct, but sometimes this happens faster than it should. It's sad to say, but many times it's things humans do that make animals become endangered or extinct.

One reason great hammerhead sharks are endangered is because people kill them and cut off their fins to make shark fin soup. If you ever see Shark Fin Soup on a menu, DON'T ORDER IT! If no one eats it, no one will kill them for their fins. Together we can slow down their extinction.

IDENTIFICATION:

You can identify the great hammerhead from other hammerheads by its almost straight hammer-shaped head that has a small indentation in the middle.

PREDATORS:

A predator is an animal that hunts, catches, and eats other animals. The animal it eats is called its prey. Juvenile (young) great hammerheads are eaten by larger sharks such as bull sharks. Adult great hammerheads have only one predator—killer whales, who hunt hammerheads of any age.

DIET

They prey on stingrays, crustaceans (crabs, shrimp) smaller fish, octopuses, and squid—not humans.

OTHER GREAT HAMMERHEAD FACTS:

- They can grow up to 6 meters/20 feet long.
- They can weigh as much as 454 kilograms/ 1000 pounds.
- They can live up to 40 years old.
- They have as many as 42 pups at a time.

DO IT!

- Mark off 6 meters/20 feet on the floor to see how long a great hammerhead could be.
- If you're having trouble with a bully, please talk to an adult who can help you.

GOOGLE IT!

1. How many other types of hammerhead sharks can you list?
2. Why are their eyes and nostrils on each end of their head?
3. What other animals are endangered?
4. Pick an endangered animal and find out how people are working to help them.
5. Are there endangered animals where you live? Can you help?
6. Where would you go if you wanted to find shark's teeth?

Go to www.Carousel-Publishing.com for free activity pages!

About Sharon Thayer, the author: Sharon's journey from dyslexic, non-reading child to national award-winning author has been an adventure filled with all the dramatic twists and turns of a great story. In one delightful chapter, she owned a nature-based kid's center/summer camp in the mountains of Colorado, where she discovered her passion for exploring the wonders of nature.

Today, Sharon entertains and inspires children of all ages through her stories that travel to magical worlds and down paths of self-discovery. Other books by Ms. Sharon: *The Story of Santa's Beard, If You Tell Me, I Can Fly! A Tooth Fairy Named Mort,* and *To the Ends of the Earth.*

About Connor Thayer, the coauthor: By nine years old, Connor had spent a third of his life begging his grandmother Sharon to write a shark book together. Side by side they researched sharks, dove into their creativity, and worked with the artists to publish this book together. Now, with "author" under his belt Connor is turning his focus to the guitar.

About Reuben McHugh, the illustrator:
As a child, Reuben picked up a passion for illustration from the influences around him; his parents who both went to Art school and his favorite children's books, mainly Dr. Seuss and Richard Scarry. He studied Art and Design at Bradford and Lincoln Colleges. After leaving college in 1989 Reuben settled into a job in the greetings card industry and it was there that his passion for illustration really took over.

About Andrew Smith, the backstory illustrator:
Andrew was born in Liverpool and grew up in this abundantly creative city. Discovering he had a talent for drawing, he studied graphic design at Liverpool University. He went on to build a career illustrating greeting cards and more recently, children's books. Andrew now lives in West Yorkshire, England with his family and enjoys hill walking in his free time.